This book belongs to

. . . .

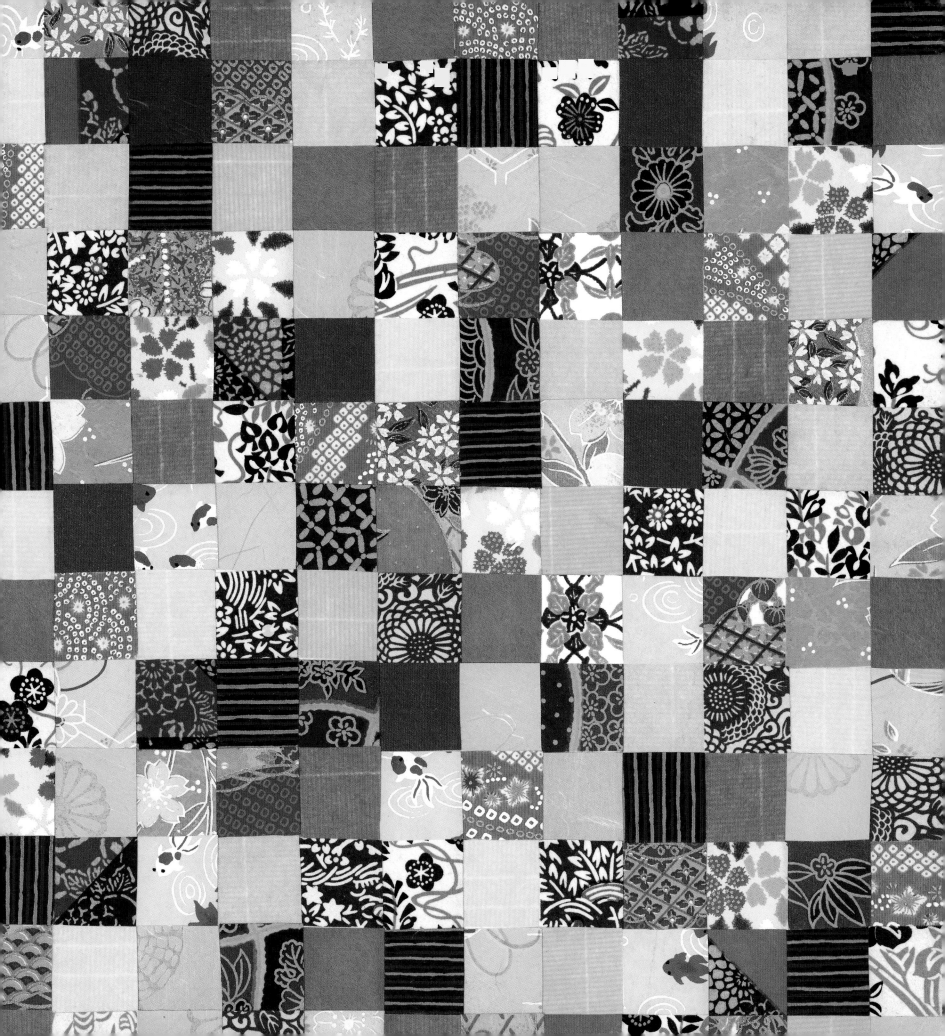

To Brian and Sue, for all your help – PB

To Nona – MM

Other books by Peter Bently & Mei Matsuoka:
THE GREAT DOG BOTTOM SWAP

First published in Great Britain in 2011 by Andersen Press Ltd, 20 Vauxhall Bridge Road, London SW1V 2SA

British Library Cataloguing in Publication Data available.

Colour separated in Switzerland by Photolitho AG, Zurich.

Printed and bound in Singapore by Tien Wah Press

Colour separated in Switzerland by Photolitho AG, Zurich.

ISBN 978 1 84939 384 3 (paperback)

10 9 8 7 6 5 4 3 2 1

The Great Sheep
Shenanigans

Peter Bently & Mei Matsuoka

ANDERSEN PRESS

"A lamb for my supper will taste mighty fine!"
Thought a wily old wolf by the name of Lou Pine
As he sneakily, slyly snuck up on the flock –
But it wasn't the sheep that were in for a shock.

He chuckled,

"How stunningly cunning I am!"

As he slunk through the hedge and met . . .

Rambo the Ram.

"Scram!" bellowed Rambo.

"Vamoose! Steer clear!

Wolves are NOT welcome!

Buzz off out of here!"

"What I need," grumbled Lou, "is a sheepy disguise
To give those dumb muttons a nasty surprise!"

So he wrapped himself up in a fluffy white gown

That belonged to Ma Watson, the best shot in town.

He lay on the road . . .

. . . to get covered in gunk.

"Baa-ha!" laughed the sheep. "It's an overgrown skunk!"

At the fair Lou saw folks eating floss on a stick.

"A fleece out of floss! What a fabulous trick!"

He flicked on the switch, and at first it was fun,

But faster
and **faster** and
FASTER

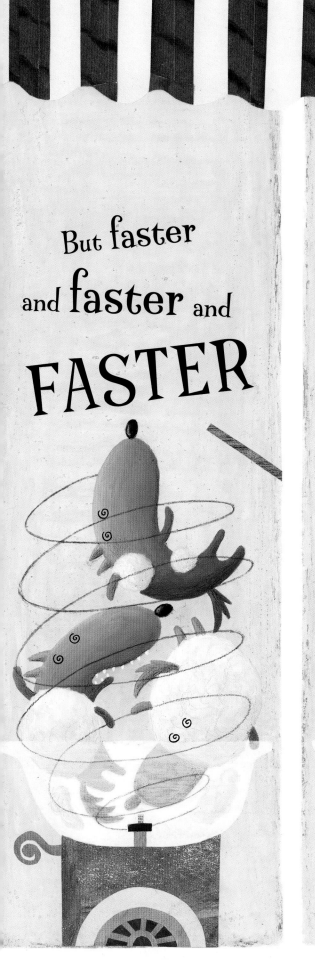

he spun . . .

He looked in the mirror
and felt his heart sink.
He'd ended up dizzy,

and sticky,
and PINK!

Lou found a thicket of blossoming trees.

Down
came
the

blossom

and down came the bees!

"I know!" spluttered Lou.
"I've a brilliant plan!
It's time for a trip to
Red Riding Hood's gran!"

"Hello, Granny dearest! It's me, Little Red!"
"My word, what a **big ball** of wool!" Granny said.

Lou dropped his hood and declared, "All the better
For you to get cracking and knit me a sweater!
And if it's not done by the time I get back
I'm just in the mood for a Gran-flavoured snack!"

The very next day Lou returned for a fitting
And had to admit Gran was dandy at knitting.
He chuckled, "How smashingly dashing I am!

Tonight I'll be scoffing a tasty young lamb!"

But Gran thought,
"He'll pay me for knitting that woolly!
I'll play my own trick on that nasty big bully!"
While Lou wasn't looking,
she grabbed a loose thread
And tied it at once to the end of her bed . . .

As he slipped through the hedgerow, some ewes standing near

Looked up at old Lou and said, "Morning, my dear!

Can you check on our lambs? They're behind that big tree."

"No problem," said Lou. "You can leave them to me!"

"I fooled them!" thought Lou. "What a genius I am!

Now shall I have cutlets? Or roast leg of lamb?

Or chops and mint sauce? Or even lamb stew?

Or burgers? Moussaka? Or lamb vindaloo?"

He hungrily hurried as far as the tree,
And peered all about, but no lambs could he see.
"They must be here somewhere. They can't have gone far.

Come out, little lambkins, wherever you are!"

And then he heard footsteps.

"Aha! Here's a lamb!"

So Lou looked around and saw . . .

Rambo the Ram.

He aimed his big horns at the wolf's derrière

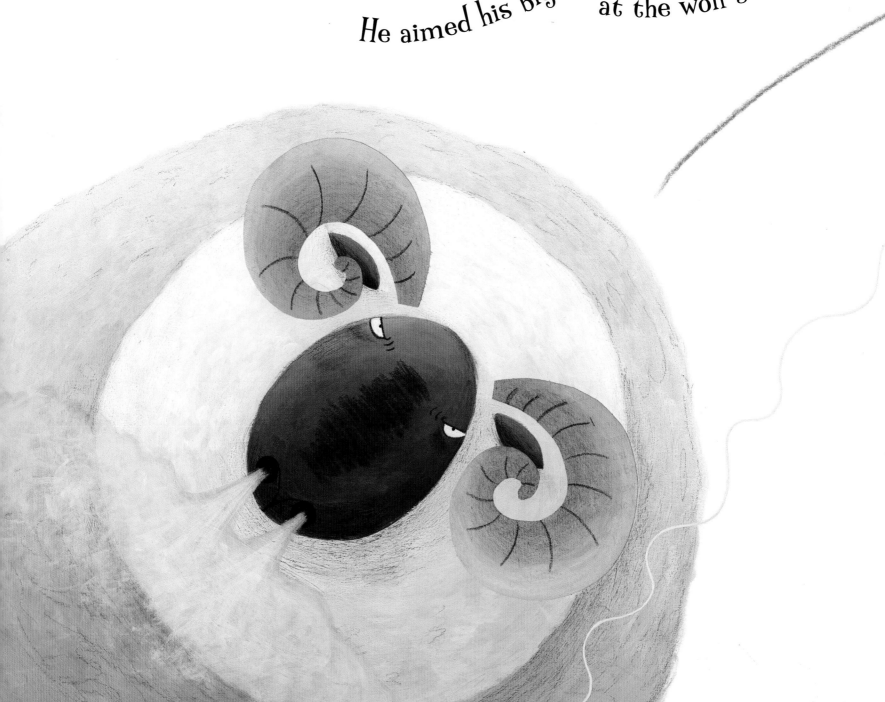

And sent him skedaddling up in the air.

"Ouch! My behind!" howled Lou as he flew...

And landed kersplat

in a big pile of poo!

"I think that's the last of the wolf and his wiles,"
Laughed Rambo. "From now on we'll smell him for miles!"

If you enjoyed this, you'll also love:

The Great Dog Bottom Swap
BY PETER BENTLY & MEI MATSUOKA
ISBN 9781842709887

'Big, clever, funny.' SUNDAY TELEGRAPH

Burger Boy
BY MEI MATSUOKA
ISBN 9781842705377

'Its witty rhymes and sprightly illustrations will definitely entertain everyone.' EVENING STANDARD

Footprints in the Snow
BY MEI MATSUOKA
ISBN 9781842707333

'A distinctive and original delight!'
SCHOOL LIBRARIAN